Penguin Island

Coral Ripley

Special thanks to Sarah Hawkins.
For Rowan Malloy.

ORCHARD BOOKS

First published in Great Britain in 2020 by The Watts Publishing Group

1 3 5 7 9 10 8 6 4 2

Text copyright © Orchard Books, 2020
Illustrations copyright © Orchard Books, 2020

A CIP catalogue record for this book
is available from the British Library.

ISBN 978 1 40836 000 2

Printed and bound in Great Britain by Clays Ltd, Elcograf S.p.A.

The paper and board used in this book are made from wood from responsible sources.

Orchard Books
An imprint of
Hachette Children's Group
Part of The Watts Publishing Group Limited
Carmelite House
50 Victoria Embankment
London EC4Y 0DZ

An Hachette UK Company
www.hachette.co.uk
www.hachettechildrens.co.uk

 Contents

Chapter One

"Are you done yet?" Layla squirmed as her big sister clipped a huge gold ring to her ear.

"I would be if you'd stop wriggling!" Nadia said.

"I can't, I'm too excited!" Layla said, grinning.

"Finished!" Nadia said. "Go and look." Layla ran over to her sister's full-length

mirror and laughed out loud. She was
dressed like a pirate in shorts and a blue-
and-white stripy top. Her dark hair was
in a long plait and, as well as the huge
earring, Nadia had
tied a skull-and-
crossbones bandana
around her head.

"Just one more
thing!" Nadia said,
pinning a colourful
toy parrot to Layla's
shoulder.

Layla gave a
happy twirl. Her
costume looked

brilliant! All month long, her school
had been learning about the secretive
smugglers and fearsome pirates that had
once hidden stolen treasures in the sea
caves near Sandcombe. Today there
was a pirate festival on the seafront, and
everyone was invited!

"Yo ho ho!" Layla sang, throwing up
her arms and doing a pirate jig in front of
the mirror.

"I thought you were in a rush?" Nadia
said, laughing.

Layla hugged her sister goodbye and
ran downstairs. It was a beautiful sunny
day, and she could smell the sea and
hear the seagulls squawking as she went

down the cobbled street to the seafront. The whole promenade by the beach had been taken over by little tents and stalls of all kinds. Colourful bunting fluttered in the breeze, and on the pier a band was playing jaunty pirate songs. Layla did another jig as she went to find her two best friends.

Spotting the first-aid tent, she popped in to say hello to her mum and dad. They were both doctors, and they'd volunteered to help out at the festival.

"Keep still for just one second—" her mum was saying to a little boy. As Layla went over, she saw that it was Henry, her friend Grace's little brother. Grace and

her mum were there too, chatting with Layla's parents.

"No more sword fighting for you, cabin boy," Layla's mum said as she bandaged up Henry's eye.

"He hit himself with his own sword!" Grace said, giggling as she came over to Layla. She was wearing raggedy trousers, a top with a skull-and-crossbones on it and she had a red bandana covering her blonde hair.

"Well, all the best pirates have eye patches," Layla joked.

"Can Layla and I go and find Emily, Mum?" Grace asked her mother.

She nodded. "Have fun, girls."

 12

"Don't get into any swordfights!"
Layla's mum called after them.

Grace and Layla giggled as they went
out into the festival. Luckily, they knew
exactly how to find Emily – by following
the delicious smell of baking! Emily's
parents owned the Mermaid Café, and
they were running a stall selling their
tasty cakes and treats.

. Emily waved as she saw her friends
coming. She was wearing a stripy dress
and had a tricorn captain's hat over her
curly black hair.

Her mum waved, too. "How *ARRRR*
you?" she asked them. "You landlubbers
look hungry. Be you wanting to feast

on our fine vitals?" She pointed at a display of cupcakes. Some had pirate faces made out of icing and others had pretty mermaids swimming in swirly buttercream frosting.

"She means, do you want a cake?" Emily said.

"Ooh, yes, a mermaid one please," Layla said as Grace nodded.

"I thought you'd choose pirate ones today," said Emily's mum, handing them their cakes.

Layla glanced at her best friends and grinned. They would always choose mermaids – because they WERE mermaids, some of the time at least!

 14

Layla smiled as she remembered the
day when she and her friends had met
a real mermaid named Marina who
had taken them to Atlantis – a magical
underwater world! To everyone's surprise,
Emily, Grace and Layla had been chosen
as Sea Keepers, whose job it was to find
the Golden Pearls. An evil siren called
Effluvia was trying to use the pearls'
magic to take over the mermaid kingdom
– and it was up to Layla, Grace and
Emily to stop her!

Layla glanced down at her shell
bracelet, wishing it would glow. As
soon as it did, they'd be off on another
mermaid adventure. Until then, at least

there was the fun festival to explore!

Munching their cakes, the girls went off to see what else they could find. There was a tombola, a ring toss and a coconut shy. They spotted Henry and Grace's mum at a stall selling treasure chests full of sweets. Henry was delightedly showing off his eye patch to his friends as he spent his pocket money. The girls waved as they went past.

At the end of the harbour, bobbing up and down on the waves, there was a real pirate ship! Layla stared up at the tall mast with the skull-and-crossbones flag flying high overhead.

"Look what it's called!" Emily gasped.

Layla narrowed her eyes. She had dyslexia, so reading was harder for her than the other. *Si-ren So-ng*, she sounded out the words. Siren Song!

Layla shuddered. Sirens like Effluvia were bad mermaids. Instead of protecting the sea, they used their powerful magic to control sea creatures and make them do whatever they wanted!

"If they knew how nasty sirens were they'd change the name!" Emily said.

"Come on." Grace pulled her friends away. "Don't worry about Effluvia. Let's have some fun!" She dragged the others on to the next stalls.

"Ooh, look! Face painting!" Layla squealed. The girls ran over to the tent. There was a plastic folder with loads of different designs to pick from.

"I might get the sparkly tiara," Emily said with a grin.

"I'm going to have a glittery seahorse," Grace said.

"I can't decide!" Layla said. But as she

turned the page, she noticed something even more exciting than the face paints. Her bracelet was glowing!

"Look!" she gasped. Layla, Grace and Emily grinned at each other, then ducked out of sight around the back of the face-painting tent. No time would pass while they were having a mermaid adventure, but they didn't want anyone to see the

magic whisking them away.

They held hands and said the magic words together.

"Take me to the ocean blue,
Sea Keepers to the rescue!"

Bubbles of magic swirled all around them, then suddenly they were in the sea – with mermaid tails instead of legs!

Chapter Two

"We're mermaids again!" Emily cheered, flipping her golden tail happily. Grace did a twirl in the water, the tiny scales on her pink tail catching the light and glinting as she swam.

Layla was using her turquoise tail to tread water as she looked around her. "Marina!" she called happily, waving to their mermaid friend.

Marina swam up to them. Layla couldn't help grinning as she saw the mermaid princess's pinky-purple hair and lilac tail.

"I'm so glad you're here!" Marina said. Layla felt a thrill as she wondered where the mermaid magic had taken them this time. She looked around, trying to work it out. The seabed was

rocky and the warm water was full of
fish. Layla watched as a shoal of black
fish with white collars and bright yellow
tails swam by, moving together like a
troupe of underwater dancers. But before
she could ask Marina where they were,
Emily started telling her about the pirate
festival.

"We were just about to get our faces
painted!" she said. "There were some
amazing designs with glitter on them."

Marina suddenly looked upset.

"What's wrong?" Emily asked her.

"It's just . . . glitter is really bad for the
sea," Marina told them.

"Is it?" Layla gasped.

 23

Marina nodded sadly. "Glitter is just tiny bits of shiny plastic. It looks pretty, but it washes into the rivers and seas, where fish swallow it. Lots of glitter ends up in sea creatures' tummies."

"I'm so sorry," Emily said, exchanging horrified looks with her friends. "We didn't know that."

"We'd never do *anything* to hurt sea creatures," Grace said firmly.

Layla felt her tummy turn over as she realised how easy it was for people to accidentally hurt sea creatures. *That's why being a Sea Keeper is so important!* she thought. "When we get home we'll tell everyone we know not to use glitter any more," she promised Marina.

Marina gave them all a big hug.
"Thank you, girls. Anyway, I didn't call
you here to talk about glitter."

"Has the Mystic Clam remembered
where another Golden Pearl is?" Grace
asked.

The Mystic Clam lived in the palace at
Atlantis. The ancient creature was the
only one old enough to remember where
the pearls had been hidden.

Marina nodded. "He gave me a new
riddle:

In a lagoon where pirates hid gold,
The golden pearl you will behold."

"Pirate gold!" Layla gasped. She

 25

couldn't believe it – they'd just been at the pirate festival and now they were looking for pirate treasure!

"What's a lagoon?" Grace asked.

"It's a bit of the sea cut off from the rest of the water," Marina explained. "It's like a big lake full of sea water. But I don't know where the nearest one is."

"Let's ask them," Emily suggested. She pointed to some dark shapes speeding through the water – penguins! "If we can catch them," she added.

The penguins twisted and spun through the water, scattering a school of red fish.

"Sorry!" Layla called to the fish as the Sea Keepers chased after the penguins.

"Well, I never!" said a red fish crossly as it darted out of the girls' way.

The penguins swam down to the rocky seabed, bubbles streaming out from their feathers, as if they were powered by tiny jet packs!

"Are they lost?" Layla asked. "I thought penguins live in cold places, like Antarctica?"

"Most do." Marina nodded. "But there is one type of penguin that lives in the Northern Hemisphere."

 28

"I bet Emily knows about it!" Layla teased her animal-loving friend.

"Is it the Galapagos penguin?" Emily asked hesitantly. She knew loads about animals from watching nature programmes on television.

"That's right!" Marina grinned. "They live by the Galapagos islands, off the coast of South America – that's where we are! But they're endangered and very rare. There aren't many left."

"Excuse me!" Layla called as a penguin shot by her, flippers flapping as if it was flying through the air. "Do you know—" Layla started, but the penguin was gone before she could finish her sentence.

29

"I've got an idea!" Grace said. The next time a penguin swam near, she put two fingers in her mouth and gave a piercing whistle. The penguin turned to look at her in surprise.

"It works on my dog Barkley," Grace whispered to the others with a giggle.

The penguin stopped and swam in front of them curiously. Then he spotted Marina's crown and did a funny little bow.

"Your Royal Highness!" he said. "I am Pedro the penguin, at your service. How may I be of assistance?"

"Thank you, Pedro," Marina said. "Do you know if there's a lagoon nearby?"

 30

"Of course, that's where the Penguin
Paddling Pool is!" Pedro said.

The girls looked at each other. That
sounded promising!

"It would be my honour to escort you
there. Right this way!" Before they could

 31

reply, the penguin shot away through the water.

Layla laughed. They were off again! "Follow that penguin!" she yelled.

Chapter Three

Pablo zipped through the water with Marina and the girls racing after him. Grace and Marina followed him easily, but Emily and Layla lagged behind, breathless. The little penguin was so fast!

Pablo led them up to a wall of black rock. When she looked at it closely, Layla noticed a narrow opening.

"This way, ladies, if you please," Pablo

 33

said, doing his funny little bow, then speeding on through the gap.

Layla laughed as she swam through the crevice and felt a burst of bubbles pop on her face.

"Mermaid magic!" Grace murmured as she came through the gap after her. The mermaids sometimes used magic bubbles to keep their world hidden from human eyes.

Once they were all through, they followed Pablo up to the surface. Layla pulled her wet hair out of her eyes and blinked in the sunshine. They were in a huge lagoon, surrounded by black rock and filled with turquoise water. At one

end of the lagoon the water was much
lighter, and the girls could see a crescent-
shaped beach. Sitting on the sand with
her tail in the water was a beautiful older
mermaid with white hair and a dark
green tail. Gathered around her were a
crowd of baby penguins, flapping their
flippers and splashing happily!

"Welcome to the Penguin Paddling Pool!" Pablo said, leading them over to the beach. "The shallow end of the lagoon is the perfect place for youngsters to learn to swim."

"Look at the baby penguins!" Layla squealed as they swam closer.

"They're tiny!" Grace said.

"Galapagos penguins are the second smallest type of penguin," Emily told the others. "I watched a documentary on them once."

The baby chicks were light grey, instead of black like Pablo, and they had white speckled tummies. They were so sweet!

The girls swam into the paddling pool. There, the water was so shallow that the girls could sit down on the sandy floor. "It's like we're in the bath!" Layla said with a giggle.

"Hello! I'm Amaya!" the older mermaid said. One penguin chick was on her lap and two others were trying to climb over her tail.

"Get down, Felipe. Pearl, Darwin, behave!" Amaya scolded them.

"You look like you've got your fins full!" Marina joked.

"I have," Amaya said.

Layla glanced at her friends. She knew they were thinking the same thing she

 37

was. "Do you need some help?" she asked.

"That would be amazing!" Amaya said. "I have so many students at the moment!"

"We'd love to help," Emily said with a smile.

"Just tell us what to do," Grace added.

"We are at your command, Amaya." Pablo flapped his flippers. "Why, I remember coming here as a tiny chick."

Amaya grinned. "You were one of the fastest learners we ever had."

Pablo fluffed up his feathers proudly.

"Once their feathers are waterproof, we teach the baby penguins how to swim here in the lagoon," Amaya explained. "It's much safer than being out in the open ocean, where predators could eat them. It's really important that they can swim so that they can find food, and so

they don't get too hot. Could you look after the youngest penguins here in the shallows?" Amaya asked the Sea Keepers. "Then Marina, Pablo and I can go a bit deeper with the ones who are almost ready to go out into the ocean."

"I'll show them how it's done!" Pablo called, then he disappeared underwater. Marina swam off after him.

"Speckles, Pebble and Peep, you stay behind with the girls," Amaya said. "Everyone else, follow me!"

She shuffled on her bottom into the water, then dived neatly under the surface. All but three of the baby penguins followed her in.

40

Layla watched them go, then turned to her friends. The three baby penguins who had been left behind clustered together on the beach, staring at the girls curiously.

"I'm Layla, this is Emily and Grace," said Layla. A very speckled grey penguin chick waddled over to her and pecked at the end of her plait. Layla giggled and reached out to tickle the penguin's soft belly. "Let me guess, are you Speckles?" she asked.

"How did you know?" Speckles gasped.

"Because of your tummy, obviously!" the biggest chick said. "That's Peep," he said, pointing to the smallest penguin

41

with his flipper, "and I'm Pebble. I can almost swim already."

"Ooh, why don't you show me," Grace suggested. "I love swimming." Pebble splashed into the shallow water and they swam around the paddling pool, Grace watching the penguin chick protectively.

"I don't like swimming," Peep said shyly.

"We can just watch," Emily told him. She pulled herself on to the beach where Amaya had been sitting before, and the little penguin hopped on her lap gratefully.

Speckles pecked Layla's plait again. "I can hold my breath for ages. Want

 42

to see?" she
asked.

"Ooh,
yes please!"
Layla told
her. Speckles
gulped in air

until her cheeks were puffed out, then
she ducked underwater and curled her
chubby penguin body up into a ball.
There was a cloud of bubbles and then
the little penguin popped back up,
looking very pleased with herself.

"Did you see?" she asked.

"It was brilliant!" Layla said, clapping
her hands.

Soon they were all having fun. Grace
and Pebble were speeding through the
water, having a race, and Emily and
Peep cheered as Speckles and Layla
played games together.

"Splash attack!" Speckles cried,
splashing water over Layla.

"Hey!" Layla said, laughing as water
droplets sparkled in the air.

Just then, Grace and Pebble popped
up next to them, breathless and excited.

"You're pretty fast," Pebble said.

"Not as fast as you!" Grace said admiringly.

"Let's show Peep that the water's fun," Layla suggested. Grace and Pebble nodded, and they all swam over to the beach.

"Come for a swim!" Grace called.

Peep shook his head.

"Come on, don't be a baby!" Pebble told him.

"It's OK," Emily reassured the little penguin, stroking his feathers. "Everyone is scared when they try something new. But I'll help you, I promise!"

"The water's lovely!" Layla said.

 45

"Lovely is it?" came a voice from nearby. "Well, not for much longer!"

The girls turned to see a mermaid with midnight blue hair and a dark purple tail pulling herself on to a rock out in the deeper water. At the base of the rock, a strange-looking fish poked his head out of the water. He had a light hanging over his face and an ugly toothy grin.

Peep gave a squawk of alarm and pitter-pattered across the sand to hide behind some rocks, leaving a trail of wet footprints behind him.

Layla gasped. Peep was right to be scared – it was Effluvia, and her nasty pet angler fish, Fang! "You'd better hide

too," she told the other penguins in a low voice. She didn't know what Effluvia was going to do, but it was sure to cause trouble.

Speckles and Pebble waddled out of the water and Emily swam over to Layla and Grace, reaching out for their hands. Whatever Effluvia had planned, the Sea

 47

Keepers would face it together!

Effluvia gave a mocking laugh as the tiny penguins scrambled over the rocks. "Tell me, do you like algae?" she asked them sweetly.

The little penguins turned at the sound of Effluvia's voice and Layla shuddered. The siren's beautiful voice was her most dangerous weapon. All mermaids sang songs to do magic, but Effluvia's singing could enchant you to do whatever she wanted! The girls had almost been tricked by her voice before.

"What's algae?" Layla whispered to Emily.

"It's a plant, like seaweed," Emily

whispered back. "Lots of sea creatures eat it because it's very nutritious."

"Nutritious, is it?" Effluvia said, overhearing. "Then you won't mind having more of it, will you?" Laughing, she spread her arms wide and opened her mouth to sing.

"Cover your ears!" Layla yelled. The penguins covered their heads with their flippers, while the girls covered their ears.

Effluvia sang in a low voice that got higher and higher, echoing around the lagoon's rocky black walls:

Siren magic send a flood,
Of toxic algae, red as blood!

The girls gasped as red algae started

to appear at the edge of the lagoon, where the penguins learned how to swim. It started in the shallow water by the beach, then spread fast, turning the light blue water dark red.

Layla, Emily and Grace stared in horror as the algae blossomed through the water all around them.

"Bye, bye, Penguin Paddling Pool," Effluvia sneered. "My algae won't stop spreading until the whole lagoon is covered!"

Chapter Four

The three baby penguins huddled together on the rocks, looking down at the gloopy red algae covering the water.

"Ew!" said Layla, swishing her tail to try and push the algae away. "This stuff is so slimy."

"What's happening?" Marina called, appearing in the deeper water with Amaya and the other penguins. "You!"

she said as she spotted Effluvia. "I should have known."

"Lovely to see you too, Princess Marina." Effluvia gave a mocking bow. "Oh, and don't think about swimming off to look for the Golden Pearl. My new pet has got its eyes on you . . ."

The siren sang a high note and a grey triangle appeared at the surface, sending shivers down Layla's spine. A shark fin!

She ducked underwater to look. It was a hammerhead shark, with bulging eyes on each end of its huge, hammer-shaped head. Its eyes glowed with strange yellow light – because the shark was under Effluvia's spell!

When Layla
surfaced again,
Effluvia was
laughing.
"The Golden
Pearl must be
somewhere in
the lagoon, because

why else would you two-legs be here? All
I have to do is wait and you'll find it for
me! But you'd better hurry up, because
my algae is spreading fast." She chortled
and flicked her tail in the water.

"Come on!" Layla called to Emily and
Layla. The girls splashed through the
slimy algae-covered water and swam

over to the others. Amaya and Marina were looking at the Penguin Paddling Pool in dismay. It was already completely covered in red!

"What are we going to do?" Emily said desperately, washing the gloopy algae off her arms in the clean water. Layla copied her, rinsing her tail. The thick red algae was in her scales and in her hair. It was horrible!

"Is there any other way to get rid of the red algae?" Grace wondered aloud.

"Can something eat it, or . . ."

Amaya shook her head. "Nothing can eat this type of algae; it's poisonous."

"Poisonous!" Layla squeaked. "It's all over me!"

"It's OK if you touch it," Amaya explained. "But if sea creatures eat it they'll get really sick. If we don't get rid of it soon, nobody will be able to live here. The whole lagoon will be ruined, for ever!"

"If we get the Golden Pearl, we can use its magic to put the lagoon back to normal," Emily said.

"We just need to figure out the riddle," Layla said.

"Do any of you know where we could find some pirate gold?" Grace asked. "That's where the Golden Pearl is hidden."

Amaya was surrounded by Pedro and the young penguins. They bobbed all around her, looking worried.

"I'm ever so sorry, but I don't know anything about pirate gold," said Pedro.

Amaya shook her head. "The lagoon is really big and deep. There are lots of places that have never been explored. But I know someone who might be able to help – Floreana."

"Is she a mermaid?" asked Emily.

Amaya laughed. "No, she's a giant

tortoise. Her family have lived by the lagoon for generations. If anyone knows about pirates, it'll be her. But she lives inland. The trail is right up there." She pointed to a rocky path along the side of the lagoon. "There's no way we can get to her, I'm afraid," she said, flipping her fins sadly.

"Well, that's OK!" Grace laughed. "Because penguins aren't the only *two-legs* around here! Marina, can you make us human again?"

Marina nodded. "I'll stay here and help Amaya with the penguins." She glanced at the red algae, which was creeping towards them. "But hurry!"

"We will," Layla promised. They swam over to the side of the lagoon and pulled themselves up on to the rocks.

Marina nodded, then opened her mouth and sang a beautiful song to turn them human again:

Water magic from the lagoon,
Make these girls human soon!

The water around them shimmered, turning their tails magically back into legs. Grace clambered to her feet and helped pull the others up. Now they were all wearing pretty summer clothes and jelly shoes that matched the colours of their tails. It felt much hotter out of the water. Layla looked at the little penguins

over on the rocks. How long could they
last in the sun without the lagoon water
keeping them cool? They *had* to find the
pearl!

"You're not fooling me, Sea Keepers,"
Effluvia shouted over to them from
her rocky perch. "That pearl must be
underwater because it was hidden by
a mermaid. I know it's in the lagoon
somewhere!"

Layla ignored her. "Come on," she said

to her friends. "Let's find Floreana."

The girls scrambled over the rocks and on to the path Amaya had pointed out. They had to push through bushes and trees as they went. It was as if they were the only people that had ever been there. *Maybe we are*, Layla thought with a jolt of excitement.

They followed the path in the baking sun. Layla was soon hot and tired. "Phew, I wish we were back at the lagoon," she said, thinking of the cool water longingly.

"I really hope Peep, Speckles and Pebble are OK," Emily said, her voice full of concern.

The thought of the penguins gave Layla a new burst of strength. They had to help them!

"There's a clearing up ahead," Grace called. She ran on – then stopped in surprise. "Whoa!" she said.

Layla and Emily skidded to a halt behind her. Layla gasped. "I know Amaya said Floreana was a giant tortoise, but I didn't think she'd be *this* big!" she whispered, staring at the huge creature in the clearing in front of them. All three girls could have sat on the tortoise's back with lots of room to spare.

The tortoise's wrinkly brown neck was stretched out as she ate leaves off a bush.

"Hello, are you Floreana?" Layla asked.

"Who wants to know?" the elderly turtle replied, still chewing. She finished her mouthful and started to move away, incredibly slowly.

Layla followed her. "We're the Sea Keepers," she explained. "We're looking for a Golden Pearl. The Mystic Clam said that there was one here at the lagoon."

"The Mystic Clam?" The tortoise stopped and gave a barking laugh. "My goodness, he knew my great-great-grandmother. I can't believe he's still around. I've heard stories about him since I was a hatchling, and that was . . . well, that was a good long while ago."

"How old are you?" Layla blurted without thinking. "Oh, I'm sorry, I don't mean to be rude."

The tortoise turned slowly and peered at the girls with her great wrinkly head. Her eyes twinkled with mischief. "It's been a long time since anyone came to visit me, and no one has ever come all the way here to insult me before!" she said, chuckling. "But if the Mystic Clam sent you, I suppose you must be OK. What do you need to know?"

"We need to find a pirate treasure," Grace told her.

"Pirates!" the old tortoise shouted angrily. "They used to eat giant tortoises, did you know that? They would take us on their ships and have us for dinner on the journey home." She shuddered. "They captured so many of my ancestors that we almost died out."

"I'm so sorry." Emily stroked her huge shell. "That must have been awful."

"Don't worry, we had our revenge," Floreana said, her eyes twinkling again.

"My great-great-grandmother scared the pirates away from the islands by making them think they were haunted. She even hid one of their maps. They had a huge treasure hidden deep in the lagoon, but they could never find it again!" She chuckled.

"We need to find that treasure to get the Golden Pearl!" said Grace excitedly. "Please can you show us where the pirates' map is?"

"Hmmm . . ." The tortoise smacked her lips together thoughtfully.

"We're not like them," Emily told her.

"We're Sea Keepers," said Layla. "We promised to help all sea creatures."

65

"Please! Toxic algae is spreading across the lagoon," Grace added. "Finding the Golden Pearl is the only way to save it."

"I'm sorry." The giant tortoise shook her head slowly. "But I'm afraid the map is lost. There is no way to find the pirate treasure!"

Chapter Five

Layla, Grace and Emily looked at each other in horror. If they couldn't find the pirate treasure, how could they get the Golden Pearl and save the lagoon?

"We'll just have to search the whole lagoon," Grace said determinedly. "We know the treasure is down there somewhere – we'll have to find it before the algae covers it all."

 67

They glanced back at the water. There was even more algae now, turning the lagoon from blue to red.

As she looked out towards the lagoon, something else caught Layla's attention. A bird was hopping about, flapping her wings frantically. "Oh no!" she called out. "Oh no, oh no, oh no!"

"Do you think she's OK?" Emily asked.

The old tortoise rolled her eyes. "She's just a silly booby."

"That's not a very nice thing to say!" Layla told Floreana. Then she felt bad. Her mum always said that she should respect her elders, and the giant tortoise was one of the oldest creatures she'd ever met! She turned to see if the old tortoise was cross. But Floreana was laughing so hard her shell shook.

"A blue-footed booby is a type of bird," she said with a wheezy laugh. "She's called Gloria."

Layla looked at the bird closely. Gloria did have the most amazing pale blue feet. But she still looked really upset.

Layla glanced at the lagoon, then back at the bird. "We have to help her," she said. "Our Sea Keeper promise was to help all sea creatures, and that means sea birds too."

Grace nodded in agreement. "But we'll have to be quick."

They raced over to where Gloria was
flapping around. "Oh dear! Oh dear!" she
squawked.

"What's wrong?" Emily asked.

"My eggs!" Gloria said anxiously.
"Have you seen my eggs?"

The girls shook their heads.

"But don't worry, we'll help you find
them," Layla promised the booby.

"They're not in my nest!" Gloria
twisted upside down and peered through
her legs. "And I can't remember where I
put them."

"Your nest? But aren't nests in trees?"
Layla looked at Emily, puzzled, but her
friend just shrugged.

"Yes, my nest!" Gloria pointed a wing at a white circle on the rocky floor.

"Ask her what it's made out of," the tortoise whispered mischievously.

"Er, what's your nest made of?" Layla asked the booby curiously.

"Well, poo, of course. What else would you make a nest out of?" Gloria said, flapping her wings crossly.

Yuck! Layla glanced at her friends and pulled a face.

Grace and Emily looked as grossed-out as she felt!

Layla peered at the rocky floor. There were a few white circles around, and some of them had other boobies sitting on them, keeping their eggs warm. "I'm glad my house isn't made out of poo!" she whispered to her friends.

"What do your eggs look like?" Emily asked the booby.

"I made them dirty so they'd blend in with the rocks," said Gloria.

"Boobies really are very silly birds," whispered Floreana.

They started searching for Gloria's eggs. Layla looked in a patch of tufty grass near the nest. The booby followed her. "Your feet are very nice," she said, looking at Layla's aquamarine jelly shoes.

"Oh, thanks," Layla said distractedly.

Gloria shuffled her feet back and forth, pointing her toes like she was doing ballet. Layla kept looking for the eggs, but the booby continued doing her strange shuffle, putting out one foot, then the other. *Oh!* Layla suddenly realised what the funny bird wanted – a compliment!

"Your feet are beautiful too!" she said kindly. "They're a lovely shade of blue."

"Thank you, thank you!" Gloria said,

preening her feathers proudly.

Layla glanced at Gloria and suddenly had an idea. Maybe to find the eggs, she had to think like a booby! What would the silly bird have done with them? She was trying to make her eggs look like rocks . . . Layla spotted a pile of rocks nearby. There, among the stones, were three smaller, rounder shapes – the eggs!

Layla raced over to them. They were still warm. "Oh, thank you, thank you!" Gloria cried as the girls each picked up an egg and put it back carefully on the booby's nest. She sat down on them and fluffed out her feathers.

"If only we could find the pirate treasure that easily," Grace said, sighing.

"Maybe you can," Floreana said. The old tortoise looked them up and down, then pulled her head inside her shell. When she stuck it out again, there was something in her mouth!

"*Mmbl blugh cabble glund . . .*," she said.

"Pardon?" Layla said.

The tortoise dropped the object in her

mouth on the ground in front of the girls. It was a thin piece of tree bark, rolled up into a scroll. "I've been carrying this around, keeping it safe, since my grandmother gave it to me," she said.

It was the pirate treasure map!

Chapter Six

"I'm sorry I lied," the tortoise said. "I don't trust humans – you wouldn't either if you were me. But you helped that silly booby, just like you said you would." She nodded her wrinkled head as she looked at them, serious for once. "I trust you, Sea Keepers."

"When we find the pearl we'll give the map straight back to Amaya and

 77

she'll make sure to get it to you," Grace promised.

"We won't let you down," Layla told the tortoise.

Emily picked up the scroll and untied it. "Goldtooth's Treasure!" she read. There was a picture of the lagoon, with the Penguin Paddling Pool at the shallow end. And at the other end of the lagoon, in the deep water, past a triangular-shaped rock and a picture of an eye, there was an X.

"X marks the spot!" Grace said breathlessly. "That must be where the pirate treasure is."

"The pirates were taking the treasure

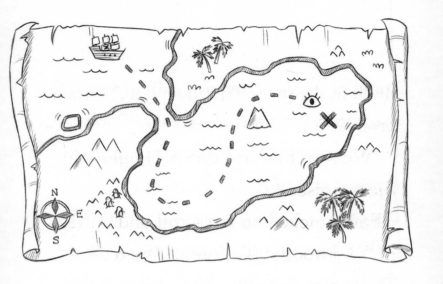

across the lagoon to bury it on the beach when the boat sank," Floreana explained. "Most of the pirates swam to shore, and they made this map to remember exactly where they'd lost the treasure." Her eyes twinkled with mischief. "But my great-great-grandmother stole it when they weren't looking."

As Layla peered at the map, Gloria

 79

came and looked over her shoulder. "Oh no, you don't want to go there!" she said with a shiver. "There are scary monsters on that side of the lagoon. Stay here instead."

"We have to go," Grace explained to the booby. "Finding the treasure is the only way we can save the lagoon."

"Thank you for your help, Sea Keepers!" Gloria said as she settled back down on her eggs. "Be careful! If I can ever do anything for you in return, just call me like this!" She gave a high whistling sound that echoed off the nearby rocks.

"Thank you, that's very kind," Layla

 80

told her, trying to copy the bird call.

"Not bad," said Gloria.

"Thank you so much," Emily said,
patting the tortoise's great shell.

The girls hugged Floreana goodbye,
then they rushed back to the lagoon.
As they got closer, Grace grabbed her
friends and pulled them down among the
rocks. "We can't let Effluvia see us," she

whispered. "If she does, she'll follow us right to the treasure."

In the water, Marina was staring up at the path anxiously, looking for any sign of them. The horrible red algae had almost reached the spot where she and the others were waiting.

Layla peeked out from behind a rock. Marina spotted her and waved, but Layla shook her head in warning. When Effluvia was looking the other way, the

girls slipped back into the water.

Marina sang the song to turn them back into mermaids and Layla felt the magical bubbles surround her. She flipped her tail excitedly. They were mermaids again!

"Let's go," Layla whispered to Marina. "First we need to find a triangular-shaped rock at the other side of the lagoon."

But just as they were about to dive underwater, Amaya and the penguins popped up to the surface. "Sea Keepers!" Pablo called, flapping his flippers in the air. "You're back!"

"Shhhh!" Emily hushed him, but it was too late. Effluvia had heard him!

"Follow those girls," Effluvia commanded her hammerhead shark. "Don't let them out of your sight and they'll lead you right to the pearl!"

The shark's fin sped through the water, heading right for them.

"What are we going to do?" Emily whispered.

"I've got an idea!" Layla said. She did the booby's call, hoping that Gloria would hear it.

For a second, nothing happened, then there was a flash of white and blue in the sky. Gloria appeared overhead.

"Do you need help?" she asked.

"Yes!" Layla said gratefully. "Can you

please distract that siren?"

"Of course!" Gloria flew over to where Effluvia was perched on the rock, then dive-bombed at her with an ear-splitting shriek.

"Get away from me, bird brain!" Effluvia screeched as Gloria swooped down and pecked at her hair.

"That's Effluvia sorted, now to deal with the shark!" Layla said.

The shark was coming towards them, but it wasn't the only problem – the toxic red algae was getting closer, too. Amaya and Marina helped the other penguins up on to the rocks, out of harm's way.

Just then, Grace had an idea. "When I say go, swim for that rock!" she told her friends, pointing to a triangular rock in the distance.

She grabbed a big handful of the slimy red algae in each hand and dived underwater.

The hammerhead shark swam towards them, his googly eyes moving from side to side and his mouth open, showing rows of sharp teeth.

Grace darted forward and threw the algae over one of the hammerhead's eyes. *SPLAT!* And then over the other. *SPLAT!*

"Go, go, go!" she yelled.

While the shark shook his head from side to side, trying to get the algae out of his eyes, Marina, Layla, Grace and Emily swam off. They raced to the other side of the lagoon, towards the triangular rock.

When they reached it, they swam up to the surface.

"Phew!" panted Layla, clutching her side. "Hunting for pirate treasure is exhausting."

"The algae won't hurt the shark, will it?" Emily checked with Marina.

Marina shook her head. "No, he didn't eat it," she said.

"So we're here," Grace said, spreading

the map out on the side of the triangular rock. "And the treasure is near this thing that looks like a massive eye . . ."

Emily looked around nervously. "Didn't the booby say there are monsters here? What if the eye belongs to a huge sea monster? And look!" She pointed to the map, where there was a drawing that looked like a sea monster.

"There's no such thing as sea monsters," Grace said.

"Most people think that about mermaids, too," Layla reminded her.

"Look!" Emily said again. On the other side of the rock, something was moving. As they watched in horror, a huge scaly

 89

claw appeared, then another . . .

"A sea monster!" Layla gulped.

The creature came round the rock. It had scaly black skin and tall spikes down its back, like a Mohican haircut. Its arms were long, with fierce-looking claws, and it had a thin, whip-like tail.

"Oh! It's an iguana!" Emily let out a sigh of relief.

"An ig-u-*what*-a?" Layla said. "It looks like a monster to me!"

"It's a lizard. My cousin has a pet one, well, a little one. But what's it doing in the sea?" Grace explained.

"The Galapagos Islands have marine iguanas!" Marina explained. "They look scary but they're very gentle. They eat algae, look!" Marina pointed at where the iguana was scraping green algae off the rock with his teeth.

Layla watched the iguana graze. Although he looked fierce and scaly with a huge spiky head, he was actually strangely beautiful. "I bet he did a great job scaring the pirates," she said.

91

The iguana turned and looked at her, licking his lips hungrily.

"Um, are you *sure* they don't eat people?" Layla asked Marina.

The iguana slipped off the rock and paddled towards them. Layla suddenly realised what he was looking at so hungrily. The red algae!

"Stop!" she called out. "You can't eat that – it's poisonous."

"It'll make you sick," Emily added.

"Thank you," he said in a gruff voice.

The girls quickly introduced themselves. "We're the Sea Keepers, and we're looking for a Golden Pearl," explained Layla.

"I'm Gus," the iguana told them.

"Do you know where we could find something that looks like this, Gus?" Grace pointed to the eye on the map.

"Sure, it's just round here," Gus said. "Follow me." He dived underwater, swimming with his arms and legs flat by his sides, using his long, powerful tail to move gracefully through the water.

Gus led them to a patch of deep water surrounded by a circle of rocks. It *did* look like an eye! Layla could just see something dark under the water down below.

"Thank you!" she called as they dived down excitedly.

As they swam deeper, they could see the dark shape was a sunken boat, and it was full of something glinting in a shaft of light coming from the surface – pirate treasure!

Chapter Seven

"Wow!" gasped Layla as she stared at the treasure lying on the bottom of the lagoon. There were hundreds of gold coins, an enormous chest with gems spilling out of it, and even a jewelled tiara, its diamonds gleaming as little fish darted around them.

"Look at this," Grace said, brandishing a huge, golden cutlass.

 95

Emily picked up a handful of coins. "These look so old," she said.

With a flick of her tail, Layla raced over to the tiara and put it on. It was surprisingly heavy! "I bet this belonged to a beautiful queen," she said. "Before it was stolen by pirates!" She swooped down to a chest and opened it. It was full of coins and jewels of all colours – sparkling red rubies, brilliant blue sapphires, and some purple and yellow gems that Layla didn't even know the names of.

"The Golden Pearl must be in here somewhere," Grace said. She opened a bag and a whole load of pearls spilled out. "But it might take us a while to find it."

"We can't even see it glowing among all these shining jewels," Layla added, putting on a shimmering necklace.

"Layla! Stop trying the jewellery on!" Emily scolded with a giggle.

"But they're so beautiful!" Layla cried.

"OK, OK, I'll look for the Golden Pearl."
She pushed a barrel of rum aside and
screamed. "*ARGH*!"

Behind it was a skeleton!

"It must be one of the pirates," Grace
said, peering at it. "Oh look, it's got a
gold tooth."

"So this *must*
be Goldtooth's
Treasure!"
Layla said,
remembering
what the map
had said.

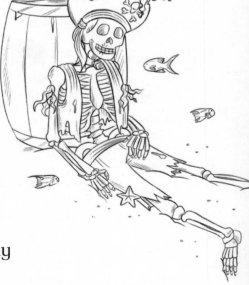

"Poor
Goldtooth," Emily

said sympathetically. "He must have died when the boat sank."

"Oh no!" Marina suddenly exclaimed.

"Do you see another skeleton?" Layla asked nervously, her heart still pounding.

"Worse!" Marina pointed through the water.

Coming towards them was the hammerhead shark. And next to it was something even scarier.

"Effluvia," Grace groaned, as the siren swam up to them.

"Yes, that's right," Effluvia drawled. "Googly-Eyes here could smell you stinky two-legs from a mile away." She sniffed delicately and sneered. "And I can smell something else – your defeat!"

The shark knocked over a chest with his tail, and swords and jewels spilled on to the seabed.

Grace swam out in front of Effluvia, still holding the golden cutlass. "We won't let you get the pearl," she said bravely.

"Oh, is that so?" Effluvia said, raising one eyebrow. She dived down and picked up a sword, a curved silver one with a black handle. Then she lunged at Grace with a fierce roar. "You two-legs are ALWAYS getting in my way!" she shouted. Grace held up her own sword and they clashed together with a clang.

Effluvia drew back and let out a

ferocious howl. Her dark-blue hair swirled in the water and her eyes looked almost black as she narrowed them at Grace. She was angrier than they'd ever seen her before.

Layla realised her friend was in real trouble. "We need to help Grace!" she cried.

Marina swam towards Grace, but Fang bit her on the tail.

"I've got her, Effluvia!" he called, his voice muffled as he held on to one of Marina's lilac fins.

"Get off me!" Marina cried, but Fang clung on tight.

Effluvia drew back her sword and

 102

whirled it overhead before attacking Grace again. "Get the pearl!" Grace yelled to Layla and Emily as her cutlass clashed with Effluvia's sword.

Layla could barely tear her eyes away from the fight, but she knew what they had to do. "Come on." She tugged Emily's arm. "We have to stop Effluvia getting the pearl."

Tearing off the heavy jewellery she was wearing so it wouldn't slow her down, Layla searched through the priceless treasures on the seabed. She and Emily scrabbled through the coins and gems, looking for the faintest glow of golden magic.

Behind them, Effluvia and Grace battled on in a fierce underwater duel. Effluvia spun the silver sword overhead and brought it down towards Grace. Just in time, Grace swept her own sword around and they met with a crash of metal. The golden sword shook in Grace's hand as Effluvia kicked her tail and pushed with all her might.

"You're. Not. Going. To. Win," Grace said through clenched teeth as she fought back.

"Shark!" Effluvia screeched. "Get those girls!"

There was only one chest left to search through, but it was locked. Emily

grabbed an oar and tried to prise it open,
as Layla tugged on the heavy lid.

"Quickly!" Layla urged. The shark was
coming closer!

As the hammerhead raced towards
them, his mouth open wide, Emily turned
and shoved the oar inside his mouth!
When the shark chomped down, his
teeth stuck fast in the oar. The shark
swam off, thrashing his head around to
try and get rid of the oar.

"That was so brave!" Layla said.

"I hope I didn't hurt it," Emily panted, swimming back down to the chest.

"It's no good, I can't get the lock open," Layla said, shaking her head.

"Do you want a hand? Or rather, a claw?" a voice drawled. It was Gus! He put one of his sharp claws in the lock and it opened with a click.

Emily and Layla heaved the chest lid and with a loud creak it burst open, showering the girls with a magical light. The Golden Pearl was inside!

Layla picked it up. The smooth pearl glowed with magical light. It was more beautiful than all the other treasure put together, and more precious, too.

"We've got it!" Emily shouted, reaching over to touch the pearl. But all three Sea Keepers needed to be touching the pearl to use its magic.

"Hurry, Grace!" called Layla.

Grace threw down her sword and swam towards the pearl.

"Nooooooo!" Effluvia screeched. The horrible siren grabbed Grace's tail!

As Effluvia clawed at her fins, Grace stretched out her fingers just far enough. The second Grace's fingers touched the pearl, Layla shouted, "Make the red algae go away!"

Chapter Eight

The girls grinned with delight as the golden light in the pearl faded away.

"Nooooo!" Effluvia howled. She let go of Grace's tail and bashed her sword on the sunken boat so hard that it broke in two. "Shark! Get them!" she yelled.

But the strange light had gone from the shark's eyes, too. Now that they'd found the golden pearl, Effluvia's spell on

 109

the shark had broken. He shook his head, looking confused.

"I can't leave it like that," Emily said.

"Be careful!" Grace called.

Emily swam up to the hammerhead and pulled the oar out of his mouth. "You were under Effluvia's spell," she said kindly.

"Thanks," said the shark, nodding his big head. Then he flicked its tail and swam off.

"Fine! I don't need you anyway, Googly-Eyes!" Effluvia shouted after him.

"Has the bad algae gone?" Gus asked.

"Let's find out!" Layla said with a grin. They swam up to the surface. The water was clear and turquoise again, and in the distance they could see the light blue water of the Penguin Paddling Pool.

"The lagoon looks beautiful again!" cried Emily in delight.

One person wasn't happy, though. Effluvia gave a shriek and pummelled the water with her fists. Then she swam up to the girls and their iguana friend. "I'll get you for this!" she screeched.

Gus stared at her blankly, then sneezed – right in Effluvia's face. "*AH CHOOO!*"

Layla, Emily and Grace couldn't help laughing as a horrified Effluvia wiped her face. "Fang!" she shrieked. "Let's get out of here!" She grabbed her angler fish and they swam off in a hurry.

"Bless you," Layla giggled as she turned
to the iguana.

"I have to sneeze to get rid of the
salt from being in the sea water," Gus
explained. "*AH CHOOO!*"

"Thank you for your help," Emily said.

"Any time!" Gus said, before sneezing
one more time.

Waving goodbye to the iguana, they went back to the shallow end of the lagoon, grinning as they swam through the clear water near the beach.

"They're back!" Peep pointed a flipper and the three little penguins raced over the rocks to greet them. Speckles gave Grace a high five.

"Thank you, Sea Keepers!" Amaya said, swimming over with the older penguins.

"Yes, jolly well done!" Pablo added. "And I'm so dreadfully sorry I alerted Effluvia to your presence."

"It's OK," Emily said kindly.

Grace handed Amaya the treasure

map. "Could you please give this back to Floreana?" she said.

"Allow me," said Pablo, bowing gallantly. "I'll bring it to her right away." He took the map in his beak and swam off to return it.

"Thank you for fixing our pool," Peep said to the girls shyly.

"You're welcome," Layla grinned. "There's only one thing that can make it better – if you have a swim!"

Peep glanced at the water, then nodded. "If you were brave enough to stop Effluvia, I can be brave enough to swim!" he said.

The girls clapped and cheered as Peep

waddled into the water. Speckles and Pebble followed, splashing each other happily. The older penguins zipped around the paddling pool, squealing in delight.

"This is great!" Peep called as he sped past. "I don't know why I was scared. Thank you so much!" He swam over to kiss Emily's cheek with his beak.

"Awww, a penguin kiss!" Layla said, grinning.

Speckles tapped Grace on the arm with her flipper. "You're IT!" she shouted, and sped off through the water, bubbles streaming out behind her.

"I'm going to get you, little penguin!"

Grace laughed as she gave chase. The girls shrieked and laughed as they played tag with the penguins. They were so fast!

Finally they all rested on the beach, panting.

"I think that's enough swimming for today," Amaya told the penguins.

"Oh!" Peep sighed, disappointed.

"You can play in the Penguin Paddling

Pool again tomorrow, thanks to the Sea Keepers!" Amaya told them.

"I think it's time for you to go too, girls," Marina said.

"Back to the pirate festival!" Emily exclaimed.

Layla gasped. She'd completely forgotten about the festival!

They hugged their penguin friends

goodbye, then Marina sang the song to send them home:

Send the Sea Keepers back to land,
Until we need them to lend a hand.

Bubbles swirled around Layla, Grace and Emily, surrounding them with mermaid magic. A moment later they were home, blinking in the sunshine. The air was filled with the sound of laughter and sea shanties, and they were dressed like pirates again.

"That was amazing!" Layla said. They walked back around to the front of the face-painting stall.

"Do you want your faces painted, girls?" the lady asked them. "I can do lots of

lovely glittery designs!"

Layla glanced at her friends. "Glitter is so pretty, but did you know it's bad for sea creatures?" she asked the lady.

"Is it?" the lady said in surprise.

Emily nodded. "When people wash off the glitter it goes down the drain and ends up in the sea. Then sea creatures eat it and it makes them ill."

"I had no idea," the lady said, picking up a packet of glitter and looking at it.

"We only just found out ourselves," Layla told her. She didn't mention that it was a mermaid who'd told them!

"Well, thank you for letting me know. I'll make sure I get some eco-friendly glitter for next time," the lady said.

Layla grinned. "We can still get our faces painted, just without glitter! I think I need a pirate beard to go with my outfit!" she joked.

"Me too!" Grace giggled. "And an eye patch!"

The girls took turns getting their faces painted, then headed back through the pirate festival, laughing each time they caught sight of each other.

"The pirate singalong is about to start on the *Siren's Song*," a voice came over the tannoy. "Join us for a sea shanty on a pirate ship, if you dare!"

Layla turned and grinned excitedly at her friends. Emily groaned. "You're going to make us sing, aren't you?" she said.

"You've defeated an evil siren and faced a sea monster," said Layla, dragging her friends towards the pirate ship. "You can't possibly be scared of a little singing."

"It wasn't really a sea monster," Emily protested. "It was an iguana."

"And you kept telling Peep he had to try new things . . ." Layla added.

"Fine!" Emily gave in, laughing.

The girls ran down the pier as the sound of sea shanties floated through the salty air. Layla glanced out at the waves, sparkling in the sunshine, and smiled. Out there in the deep water there was a magical mermaid world, and she couldn't wait to go back there again soon!

The End

Join Emily, Grace and Layla
for another mermaid adventure in …

Sea Otter Summer camp

Grace swam down and peered into the crack. It was even darker down there, and it looked like there were things scuttling about in the black water. It was a bit spooky!

Grace felt something touch her arm and jumped in alarm, then felt a bit silly when she realized it was just a bit of slimy kelp brushing against her as it moved in the tide. But then a shadow fell over her.

"Effluvia!" she shouted, her heart

beating fast as she spun around.

"It's only a sea otter!" Emily reassured her.

They looked at the little creature with its sleek brown fur and friendly face. It galloped through the water, doing a sort of doggy paddle as it swam along.

Read Sea Otter Summer Camp to find out what happens next!

How to be a real-life

Would you like to be a Sea Keeper just like Emily, Grace and Layla? Here are a few ideas for how you can help protect our oceans.

1. Try to use less water
Using too much water is wasteful. Turn off the tap when you brush your teeth and take shorter showers.

2. Use fewer plastic products
Plastic ends up in the ocean and can cause problems for marine wildlife. Instead of using plastic bottles, refill a metal bottle. Carry a tote bag when out shopping, and use non-disposable food containers and cutlery.

THANK YOU FOR USING
NORFOLK LIBRARIES
You can renew items online,
by Spydus Mobile Phone App
or by phone at 0344 800 8020
Ask staff about email alerts
before books become overdue

Self Service Receipt for Renewing Item

Name: **********6864

Title: Penguin Island

Item: 30129084419762

Due Back: 15/08/2023

Total Renewing: 0
25/07/2023 14:27:26

Norfolk Library and Information Service
Please keep your receipt

Sea Keeper

3. Help at a beach clean-up
Keeping the shore clear of litter means less litter is swept into the sea. Next time you're at the beach or a lake, try and pick up all the litter you can see.

4. Reduce your energy consumption
Turn off lights when you aren't using a room. Walk or cycle instead of driving. Take the stairs instead of the lift. Using less energy helps reduce the effects of climate change.

5. Avoid products that harm marine life
Do not buy items made from endangered species. If you eat seafood, make sure it comes from sustainable sources.

SEA KEEPERS

Dive in to a mermaid adventure!

The Mermaid's Dolphin
Coral Ripley

The Sea Unicorn
Coral Ripley

Coral Reef Rescue
Coral Ripley

Sea Turtle School
Coral Ripley

Penguin Island
Coral Ripley

Coming Soon

Sea Otter
Summer Camp
Coral Ripley

The Rainbow Seahorse
Coral Ripley

Whale Song Wedding
Coral Ripley